Copyright © 2003 by NordSüd Verlag AG, Zürich, Switzerland
First published in Switzerland under the title Das Osterküken.
English translation copyright © 2004 by North-South Books Inc., New York.

First published in the United States, Great Britain, Canada, Australia, and New Zealand in 2004 by North-South Books Inc., an imprint of NordSüd Verlag AG, Zürich, Switzerland.

First paperback edition published in 2006 by North-South Books Inc. Distributed in the United States by North-South Books Inc., New York.

Library of Congress Cataloging-in-Publication Data is available.
A CIP catalogue record for this book is available from The British Library.

ISBN: 978-0-7358-1855-2 (trade edition)
10 9 8 7 6 5 4 3
ISBN: 978-0-7358-2076-0 (paperback edition)
10 9 8 7 6 5 4 3 2

Printed in Belgium

The Easter Chick

By Géraldine Elschner

Illustrated by Alexandra Junge

Translated by Marianne Martens

NORTHSOUTH
BOOKS
New York • London

Hilda had laid the most beautiful egg, and she fussed over it lovingly. But she was getting a little worried. Weeks had passed, and still her baby hadn't hatched. Suddenly she heard a little voice. 'Mother, when is Easter?' Hilda jumped up in shock. Who could be speaking to her?

"Please, Mother, please tell me.
How many more days?"
Hilda couldn't believe it. The voice
seemed to be coming from the egg.
"Un...un...until Easter?" Hilda sputtered.
"Why I'm not sure! I know Easter is
in the spring. Sometimes it's in
March, other times in April. Each
year it changes."
"Oh, Mother, please find out for me,"
peeped the little chick. "The whole
chicken coop keeps talking about
how lovely Easter is, so I really
want to hatch on Easter Sunday.
I want to be an Easter chick."
"That certainly is an amazing
idea," said Hilda, "but why not?"
So off she went to find out.

First Hilda asked the dog. Then the cat. Then the cow.
Then the pig and, finally, the sheep. "When is Easter?"
she asked. But no one knew the answer. Not
even the bunnies. "Sorry, we're not Easter bunnies,"
they apologized. "Maybe Max can help you."

Max the owl lived in a tree behind the barn.
That night Hilda snuck out of the chicken coop
to ask Max about Easter.
"Of course I know when Easter is," said Max.
"If your little chick wants to hatch on Easter, three
things have to happen. First, she must wait for the
first day of spring. On that evening, I'll hoot once.
When you hear me, meet me by the barn."

Hilda ran back to her nest
and told her little chick what
the owl had said.

"Oh, I can hardly wait!" said
the little chick impatiently.

Finally March 21 arrived and with it came spring.
That night, a long hoot was heard across the
barnyard. *Whoooo hoooo!*
Quickly Hilda ran to the big barn.
"Your little chick still needs to be patient,"
explained Max. "She will have to
wait for the next full moon.
On that night, I'll hoot two
times. When you hear me,
meet me by the barn."

The little chick grew more and more impatient. "How will I know when the moon is full?" she said. "I can't see anything from inside this egg." So Hilda poked a tiny hole in the egg and stuck a piece of straw in so that her baby could watch the moon.

At first the moon was thin and curved like a backward letter C.

Slowly it started to take the shape of a horn.

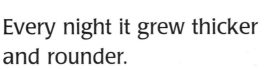

Every night it grew thicker and rounder.

"It won't be long before the full moon is here," said Hilda.

The little chick jumped for joy, making the egg wobble.

When the moon was finally full, Hilda heard Max hooting again: *Whooo hoooo! Whooo hoooo!* "Next Sunday will be Easter," said Max. "Easter is always the first Sunday after the first full moon that comes after the first day of spring."

"On the night before Easter, I'll hoot three times. Next morning, when the church bells ring, it will be Easter, and your little chick can finally hatch out of her egg."

The little chick counted down the days: Monday, Tuesday, Wednesday, Thursday, Friday. On Saturday night, there were three loud calls through the farmyard.
Whoooo hoooo!
Whoooo hoooo!
Whoooo hoooo!

On Easter morning, all the church bells started to ring at once. "Here I come!" called the little chick, happily cracking out of her egg.

"Father! Mother! Come quickly!" called the farmers'
children, who were looking for Easter eggs in the
barn. "A little chick just hatched! On Easter Sunday!
Isn't that amazing?"

Hilda and her little chick smiled at one another.
It *was* pretty amazing at that!

Then the little chick headed outside to
admire the big, bright, beautiful world.
"Happy Easter!" she called.
"Happy Easter birthday to me!"